The Catspring Somersault Flying One-handed Flip-flop

story by SuANN KISER   pictures by PETER CATALANOTTO

ORCHARD BOOKS   NEW YORK

Special thanks to Ellen Mager, Debbie Croll,
and her daughter Anna—P.C.

Text copyright © 1993 by SuAnn Kiser
Illustrations copyright © 1993 by Peter Catalanotto

Orchard Books, 95 Madison Avenue, New York, NY 10016

Manufactured in the United States of America
Printed by Barton Press, Inc. Bound by Horowitz/Rae
The text of this book is set in 16 point Plantin.
The illustrations are watercolor paintings reproduced in full color.
10 9 8 7 6 5 4 3 2 1

Library of Congress Cataloging-in-Publication Data
Kiser, SuAnn. The catspring somersault flying one-handed flip-flop /
story by SuAnn Kiser ; pictures by Peter Catalanotto. p. cm.
"A Richard Jackson book"—Half-title.
Summary: When everyone in her large family seems too busy around
the farm to pay any attention to her, a young girl decides to run
away to find someone who will watch her do her new trick.
ISBN 0-531-05493-4. ISBN 0-531-08643-7 (lib. bdg.)
[1. Family life—Fiction. 2. Runaways—Fiction. 3. Farm life—
Fiction.] I. Catalanotto, Peter, ill. II. Title.
PZ7.K6454Cat 1993 [E]—dc20   92-44519

For my grandmother Promise and her
twelve children: Alfie, Derald, Emery,
Fred, Ila, Kenneth, Lena, Lilly, Phyllis,
Thelma, Violet, and Wilma, my mother

—S.K.

For my sister Louisean

—P.C.

WILMA Letitia Carper liked doing "boy things" so much more than she liked doing "girl things" that everyone called her Willy. And that was just fine with her.

Willy lived way out in the country on a farm with her mama and papa and eleven brothers and sisters. And that was just fine with Willy too.

One day Willy did something really truly amazing, but no one paid any attention to her. And that was not at all fine with Willy.

It was a Saturday afternoon in early autumn, and everyone was in the south pasture taking a break from work.

Everyone, that is, except Willy. Willy was off in a far corner, working hard, practicing something new that only she could do. And even she couldn't do it yet.

By and by, everyone else wandered off to finish their chores.

But Willy didn't notice. She practiced and practiced.
And then she practiced some more. And suddenly . . .
Sproing–whoop–whoosh–boing–whip–whap!

She did it!

The world's first ever Catspring Somersault Flying One-handed Flip-flop!

It was the most amazing thing Willy had ever done, if she did think so herself. And she did!

"Look what I can do!" yelled Willy. But there was no one around to look.

Lickety-split, Willy ran to the house.

Thelma and Ila were baking bread and Alfie was feeding the babies.

"Watch me do my Catspring Somersault Flying One-handed Flip-flop!" said Willy.

"Just as soon as we're done," said Thelma, "which would be a lot sooner if you were to help."

Willy fed Derald and Kenneth a few bites of mashed potato. But she was too excited to stay, so when no one was looking, Willy sneaked out the back door.

Lena, Phyllis, and Lilly were in the backyard helping Mama hang clothes on the line.

"Watch me do my Catspring Somersault Flying One-handed Flip-flop!" said Willy.

"We're too busy right now," said Mama.

"Why don't you pitch in?"

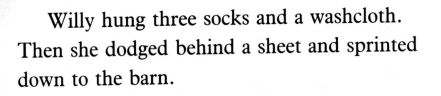

Willy hung three socks and a washcloth.
Then she dodged behind a sheet and sprinted
down to the barn.

Emery, Violet, and Fred were helping Papa tend the livestock.

"Watch me do my Catspring Somersault Flying One-handed Flip-flop!" said Willy.

"We don't have time," said Papa, "but we could use another hand."

Willy fed Beauty a handful of hay.

"Beauty, nobody in this family pays any attention to me," she muttered. "It would serve them right if they *never* got to see my Catspring Somersault Flying One-handed Flip-flop! I'll just run away and show someone else!"

And off she went, lickety-split.

Willy ran down the road to Grandpa's house. But he and his old cat Jezebel were napping on the porch, and Willy didn't want to disturb them.

She trotted to her teacher's house, but Miss James was
grading papers and told her to come back the next day.

She walked all the way to her best friend's house, but
Elaine's mother said Elaine was over at the Hackensacks'
farm helping out with the new twins.

Willy turned around and headed back home. "There's
no point in running away to show someone else my
Catspring Somersault Flying One-handed Flip-flop if there's
no one else to show," she grumbled.

Willy arrived home just as Mama rang the dinner bell. During the fried chicken, the biscuits and gravy, and the corn on the cob, no one said a word to Willy. They were even quieter during the bread pudding.

Finally Willy couldn't stand it one second longer. "I bet if I ran away, none of you would even know I was gone," she said.

Papa put down his spoon. "You would lose that bet, Willy," he said.

"If you ran away, every single one of us would know,"
said Mama.

"I would be the first to notice," said Thelma.
" 'Where's Willy?' I would ask everyone, and everyone
would say, 'She was right here a minute ago.' "

"So we would all run around calling, "*Willy! Oh, Willy!*" said Phyllis.

"Soon both babies would start yowling," said Alfie.
"And Old Watch would start howling," said Emery.

"Which would scare Beauty halfway out of her hide and all the way out of the barn," said Lilly.

"And all the other critters would get excited and chase after Beauty across the garden and through the clothes on the line," said Fred.

"And right into the parlor," said Lena.

"Where they would kick up a fearsome mess," said Ila.

"And after all was done and said, we would decide that since you caused the whole mess by running away, you should be the one to clean it up," said Violet.

"Right after you showed us your Catspring Somersault Flying One-handed Flip-flop, that is!" said Papa.

"Why, that's the silliest story I ever heard," said Willy.
But for once she had the attention of the whole family.
So, lickety-split, up she jumped, and . . .

Sproing—whoop—whoosh—boing—whip—whap!
She did the world's best ever Catspring Somersault
Flying One-handed Flip-flop right then and there in the
dining room!

Everyone clapped and cheered.

"Now, Willy," said Mama, "you must never even think of running away . . .

ever again!"

And that was just fine with Willy.